PRESENTED TO

_____

FROM

_____

DATE

_____

OTHER CROSSWAY BOOKS BY MAX LUCADO

# In the Beginning

## Max Lucado

CROSSWAY BOOKS • WHEATON, ILLINOIS

A PUBLISHING MINISTRY OF GOOD NEWS PUBLISHERS

PUBLISHER'S ACKNOWLEDGMENT

The publisher wishes to acknowledge that the text for *In the Beginning* appeared originally in *Tell Me the Story*, written by Max Lucado and illustrated by Ron DiCianni. Special thanks to Ron DiCianni for the idea and vision behind the creation of the "Tell Me" series. Look for more stories in the series–*Tell Me the Secrets*, *Tell Me the Truth*, *Tell Me the Promises*, and *Tell Me Why*, all published by Crossway Books–at your local bookstore.

*In the Beginning*
Copyright © 1992, 2006 by Max Lucado
Published by Crossway Books, a publishing ministry of Good News Publishers
1300 Crescent Street, Wheaton, Illinois 60187

Interior Design: Jon McGrath & Josh Dennis; Cover Design: Josh Dennis
Illustrations: Josh Dennis; Photography: Josh Dennis & Jon McGrath, Photos.com, iStock
Edited by Karen Hill
First printing 2006
Printed in Italy

ISBN-10: 1-58134-760-X

LIBRARY OF CONGRESS CATALOGING-IN-PUBLICATION DATA
Lucado, Max.
 In the beginning / Max Lucado.
    p. cm.
  Summary: An angel assists the Father as he creates, out of the great emptiness, stars and water and creatures, then uses a bit of Himself to make His children.
  ISBN 1-58134-760-X (hc : alk. paper)
 [1. Creation–Fiction. 2. God–Fiction. 3. Angels–Fiction.] I. Title.
 PZ7.L9684In 2006
 [Fic]–dc22                                    2005026674

PBI   13   12   11   10   09   08   07   06
15  14  13  12  11  10  9  8  7  6  5  4  3  2  1

For Susan Perry—
*Celebrating your tender heart*
*and devoted service*

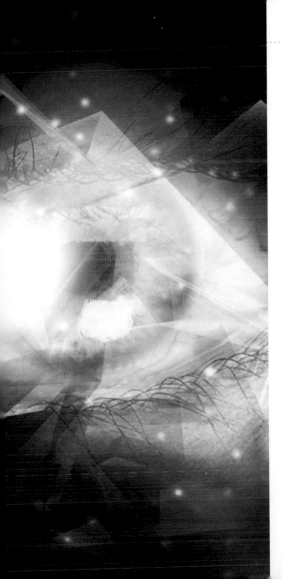

The Father was DREAMING. I could see it in His eyes–the sparkle. It was there again.

*"What is it You see, my King?"*

He didn't turn, but kept His gaze fixed on the great emptiness–the massive, boundless, unending space. The more He looked, the more His eyes would dance. I knew He saw something.

I looked in the same direction. I leaned forward and stared intently. All I saw was emptiness. All I ever saw was emptiness.

I hadn't seen the sphere that He had PULLED OUT OF THE SKY. *"Where was that?"* I asked as He began MOLDING it in HIS HANDS.

*"It was there,"* He replied, looking outward. I looked and saw nothing. When I turned, He was smiling. He knew a seraph's vision was too limited.

The same thing happened with the water. *"Where did this come from?"* I asked, touching the strange substance.

*"I saw it, Michael."* He chuckled as He filled an ocean from His palm. *"And when I saw it, I made it. I saw it near the stars."*

*"The what?"*

*"The stars."* Out into the void He reached. When He pulled back His hand, He kept it closed as if to entice me to lean forward. I did. And just as my face was near, He opened His hand. A BURST OF LIGHT escaped, and I looked up just in time to see it illuminate His face, too. Once again, He was smiling.

*"Watch how they sparkle,"* He reveled. And with a flip of His wrist, the palmful of diamonds SOARED into the blackness until they found their destiny, and there they hung.

*"Won't the children love them?"* the Maker said as together we watched the twinkling begin.

I still wasn't sure what or who these "children" were, but I knew they occupied a place in the DREAM like nothing else. Ever since the DREAM started, the Father spoke often of these children—what they would like, how they would respond.

I remember once, the Father held the sphere in one hand and motioned to me with the other. *"Come. See what the children will see."* He then put His fingers to His lips and *blew* gently. Off His fingertips floated tiny whiffs of white cotton balls of fluff.

*"What do they do?"* I asked as the train of puffs sailed toward the globe.

*"Oh, Michael,"* He boomed with excitement, *"they do everything. They give shade. They give rain. But most of all, My children can watch them pass and, if they look closely, they will see Me."*

That was the way He thought about everything. All the DREAM was for the children. And in all the DREAM was the Father. With a **waterfall**, He said, *"I made it small so they could run in and out."* With the **dandelion**: *"This is just the right size for the children to blow,"* and the **rivers** in the **canyon**: *"They can sit right here and watch the water race into the valley."*

*"But where are the children?"* I once asked, looking into the same space from whence had come the rest of the DREAM.

*"Oh, not out there,"* responded the Artist. There was urgency in His voice as He repeated, *"Not out there."*

But that is all the Father said. And that's all I asked.

With the coming of the creatures, I almost forgot. We laughed so much as He made them. Each one was special. The TINY wing for the mosquito. The HONK so unlike any other sound for the goose. The shell for the turtle. The darting eyes of the owl.

He even let me decorate a few. I put violet in the butterfly wings, and He loved my idea to s t r e t c h the elephant's nose.

What fun it was as the heavens gave birth to fowl and fish, reptile and rodent! No more had the little ones scurried off His palm than the giant ones appeared. He grabbed the giraffe and stretched its neck, and He put a hole in the whale's head ("so it will come to the surface to breathe and the children will see it").

*"What will we call them all?"* I asked.

*"I'll leave that up to the children."*

The CHILDREN—I'd almost forgotten. But He hadn't. As the last winged creature left His fingers, He turned and looked at me and I knew.

*"It's time?"*

*"Yes, it's time."*

I expected to see His eyes dance again. But they didn't. I anticipated eagerness. But He didn't begin. For a long period, He sat looking out into the void—longer than normal.

*"Do You see the children?"*

*"No. They are not to be found out there."*

*"Then what do You see?"*

*"I see their deeds."*

He spoke softly. The joy was gone from His voice.

*"What? What is it? What is it You see?"*

Perhaps it was because He thought I needed to know. Or maybe because He needed someone else to know. I'm not sure why, but He did what He had never done. He let me see. As if the sky were a curtain, **HE TOOK IT AND PULLED IT BACK.**

Before I could see it, I could smell it. The stench stung my eyes. *"It's greed you smell,"* He explained. *"A love for foolish, empty things."*

I started to turn away. But my King didn't; so I didn't. I looked again.

It was so **dark**–a **darkness** unlike the starless sky–a **blackness** unlike the void. This **darkness** moved. It crept. It **shadowed** and swayed. It was a **living soot.** He knew my thoughts and spoke.

His words were s l o w and  s p a c e d . *"They will put it out."*

*"What?"*

*"They will destroy that which makes them Mine."*

It was then I saw it for the first time. He reached into **HIMSELF**—deep into His own self and pulled it out. A flame. A shining circle.

It glowed brilliantly in His palm. Much brighter than the constellations He had spread about or the sun He'd ignited.

*"This is . . . "* I began.

*"This is a part of Me,"* He finished and added what I couldn't have imagined. *"And out of Me, I will make My children."*

For the first time I saw. I saw why the children were so TREASURED. I saw the uniqueness in them. They bore **HIS** light—the universe **HE** created, the children **HE** fathered.

*"But the darkness?"* I had to ask. *"Why?"*

*"Just as I chose, so must they choose. Else they won't be Mine."*

Just then His face lifted. His eyes brightened. *"But they won't all forget Me. Look."*

Into tomorrow I gazed. At first I saw nothing. Just swarthy darkness billowing. But then, as I searched, I saw. First, only one, then a cluster, then more–LIGHTS THEY WERE. Flickers of candles, weakened but not lost in the blackness. Like the stars He had cast against the black heavens, these flames flickered in a sable sea.

*"It's My children."* There was pride in His voice. *"My children remember."*

THE LOOK ON HIS FACE, I CANNOT FORGET. His eyes had sparkled when He suspended the planets in space; His cheeks had danced as He heard the cat purr. I had seen His face alive before—BUT NOT LIKE NOW. For at this moment—when He saw His children alight in the darkness—when He saw those who were His seeking Him—HE CELEBRATED. His countenance EXPLODED WITH JOY. His head flew back, and laughter SHOOK THE STARS.

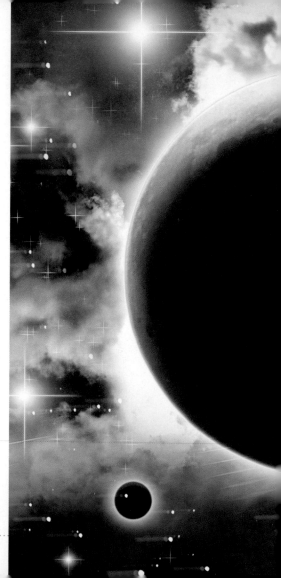

"*My children, My children, My children,*" were
His only words. And then, He paused, wiped the tears
from His face, and pledged a PROMISE for all of
Heaven to hear.

"*You haven't forgotten Me; I won't forget you.*"

Then He turned to me. "*To the work, Michael; we've
much to do. We must make the Dream come true.*"

And I thought making the animals was a delight. "*No
two will be alike,*" He vowed as He began reaching
into Himself for balls of light. "*Some big, some
small. Some timid, some bold. Some with big ears,
some with little.*" And off His palm they came.
Generation chosen. Destination determined. Each
with a different thread of character or shape of body.

But each with a bit of Him—a light within.

And He even let me help. *"Look what I made, Father,"* I told him. *"I call them freckles. Let me show You how they work."*

AND HE SMILED.

the End of the Beginning

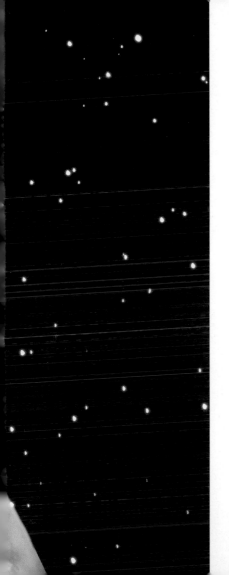

### The Beginning of Creation

1 In the beginning, God created the heavens and the earth. 2 The earth was without form and void, and darkness was over the face of the deep. And the Spirit of God was hovering over the face of the waters.

### The Six Days of Creation

3 And God said, "Let there be light," and there was light. 4 And God saw that the light was good. And God separated the light from the darkness. 5 God called the light Day, and the darkness he called Night. And there was evening and there was morning, the first day.

6 And God said, "Let there be an expanse in the midst of the waters, and let it separate the waters from the waters." 7 And God made the expanse and separated the waters that were under the expanse from the waters that were above the expanse. And it was so. 8 And God called the expanse Heaven. And there was evening and there was morning, the second day.

9 And God said, "Let the waters under the heavens be gathered together into one place, and let the dry land appear." And it was so. 10 God called the dry land Earth, and the waters that were gathered together he called Seas. And God saw that it was good.

11 And God said, "Let the earth sprout vegetation, plants yielding seed, and fruit trees bearing fruit in which is their seed, each according to its kind, on the earth." And it was so. 12 The earth brought forth vegetation, plants yielding seed according to their own kinds, and trees bearing fruit in which is their seed, each according to its kind. And God saw that it was good. 13 And there was evening and there was morning, the third day.

14 And God said, "Let there be lights in the expanse of the heavens to separate the day from the night. And let them be for signs and for seasons, and for days and years, 15 and let them be lights in the expanse of the heavens to give light upon the earth." And it was so.

·16 And God made the two great lights–the greater light to rule the day and the lesser light to rule the night–and the stars. ·17 And God set them in the expanse of the heavens to give light on the earth, ·18 to rule over the day and over the night, and to separate the light from the darkness. And God saw that it was good. ·19 And there was evening and there was morning, the fourth day.

20 And God said, "Let the waters swarm with swarms of living creatures, and let birds fly above the earth across the expanse of the heavens." 2·1 So God created the great sea creatures and every living creature that moves, with which the waters swarm, according to their kinds, and every winged bird according to its kind. And God saw that it was good. 22 And God blessed them, saying, "Be fruitful and multiply and fill the waters in the seas, and let birds multiply on the earth." 23 And there was evening and there was morning, the fifth day.

24 And God said, "Let the earth bring forth living creatures according to their kinds–livestock and creeping things and beasts of the earth according to their kinds." And it was so. 25 And God made the beasts of the earth according to their kinds and the livestock according to their kinds, and everything that creeps on the ground according to its kind. And God saw that it was good.

26 Then God said, "Let us make man in our image, after our likeness. And let them have dominion over the fish of the sea and over the birds of the heavens and over the livestock and over all the earth and over every creeping thing that creeps on the earth."

27 So God created man in his own image, in the image of God he created him; male and female he created them.

28 And God blessed them. And God said to them, "Be fruitful and multiply and fill the earth and subdue it and have dominion over the fish of the sea and over the birds of the heavens and over every living thing that moves on the earth." 29 And God said, "Behold, I have given you every plant yielding seed that is on the face of all the earth, and every tree with seed in its fruit. You shall have them for food. 30 And to every beast of the earth and to every bird of the heavens and to everything that creeps on the earth, everything that has the breath of life, I have given every green plant for food." And it was so. 3·1 And God saw everything that he had made, and behold, it was very good. And there was evening and there was morning, the sixth day.

### The Seventh Day, God Rests

2 Thus the heavens and the earth were finished, and all the host of them. 2 And on the seventh day God finished his work that he had done, and he rested on the seventh day from all his work that he had done. 3 So God blessed the seventh day and made it holy, because on it God rested from all his work that he had done in creation.